LOCK&KEY CHRISTMAS

CAT PORTER

WILDFLOWER INK, LLC

Lock & Key Christmas
Cat Porter © 2018
Wildflower Ink, LLC
All rights reserved.

Editor
Jennifer Roberts-Hall

Cover Photo
Pigoff Photography on Unsplash

Cover Design
Cat Porter

Special thanks to Christina Trevaskis, Lori Jackson, Linda R. Russell

ISBN: 978-0-9903085-9-1

Visit my website at www.catporter.eu

CONTENTS

1

MILLER

"What do you mean you don't have the presents?" Grace's voice pitched high.

"I mean, I don't have the presents," I whispered, taking off my wet jacket and hanging it in the mudroom. "The road to the club was already blocked by the time I got there."

"Say again?"

I kicked off my boots. "Baby—"

"No, no, no. You're kidding, right?"

"Wish I was."

"I was hoping you'd be able to—"

"I know."

"Oh my God. What are we going to do? What are we going to tell him?"

"Well—"

"Because you realize that whatever we tell him won't matter a hill of beans because he's a four-year-old boy who is expecting presents on Christmas. Logic and understanding do not factor into this equation. Not one bit. The only thing that matters is loads of wrapped presents under that tree for him to open."

We both turned and stared at the tree void of any brightly wrapped gifts underneath its branches.

I shifted my weight. "Is that the meaning of Christmas? Is that what we're teaching him?"

She groaned. "No, of course not, but it still doesn't change the fact that he's a little boy and the buildup to ripping wrapping paper apart and opening presents on this one day is extreme. He made his list for Santa over a month ago, and wrote it himself. And we encouraged him."

"Yeah, but we didn't promise him that he'd get everything."

"Of course we didn't, but—oh my God."

"Sweetheart, take a deep breath."

"It's Christmas Eve."

"You don't have anything here at home?"

She shook her head, her teeth scraping her gorgeous bottom lip. "I've been stashing the goods at the warehouse at work. Everything, even the small stuff—the leather bracelet, the bandana. You know how he is, he gets into everything, finds *everything*."

"That's our boy."

She tugged on her hair. "And there I was so proud of myself for having taken care of it all ahead of time—the shopping, the wrapping, the stashing it all at work. The top secret secrecy."

"And you got snowed in quicker than you expected and couldn't get them here when you'd planned."

Her eyes filled with water as she nodded. "And we won't be able to go to the midnight service at the church either which is probably canceled anyway. And Thunder was all excited to stay up late and get dressed up in his new clothes."

"Aw, baby." I brushed her forehead with my lips. "I know you want everything to be perfect for our Christmas, but twelve hours of steady, heavy snowfall in the Black Hills tends to mess with everyone's best-laid plans."

"Well, there's always baked potatoes."

"Baked potatoes?"

"In a couple of the "Little House" books, Laura and Mary and their family would inevitably get snowed in during Christmas, especially when they lived in the Dakota territory, and all the kids got for Christmas was a baked potato. And they were so grateful."

"I don't think a potato is gonna fly for Thunder."

"Me neither." She let out a laugh and pressed her hands into my chest, down to my waist. "Anyhow, the only baked potatoes in the house are currently stuffed with bacon, melted cheddar, loads of butter and cream and waiting to be paired with my filet mignon."

"Now you're talking. I've been thinking about your stuffed cheesy potatoes and steak all day."

"Hmm. Don't worry, there's plenty." She let out a sigh, giving me a soft grin which heated my flesh still chilly from the winds outside. "The important thing is that you aren't stuck in Wyoming because that would've been horrible. I was getting worried."

"I wouldn't have gone if it wasn't an emergency. The Kades are our biggest clients, and his guy managed to find that Corvette, and I was the only one he wanted touching it. Travis and I did what we could under the circumstances. That annual Christmas auction of theirs is a huge deal and huge for us. He paid me in cash this time, with an added extra for the holiday."

"Really? So you're loaded right now, Mr. Moneybags?" She patted my back pockets, squeezing my ass, and I kissed her.

"Did Travis get home okay?" she asked, wiping the damp hair back from my face.

"Yeah, this is when living in the center of town is a plus. Down there, the roads were still passable in the truck. I'm sure they aren't anymore. Speaking of which, my dad called me."

"I was expecting him, but he never showed—"

"He's not coming."

"Because of the weather?"

I shrugged, my jaw tightening. "So he said. But I'd told him to come from yesterday, but obviously he put it off. If he really wanted to come, he would have."

Over the past few years since my dad and I had started talking again, he'd say no to me more often than yes about anything—me helping him do repair work on his house, keeping up with his doctor visits after his leg surgery. Both of us had a hard time reaching each other, both of us stubborn, awkward. It was a muffled relationship, but we tried, that counted for something. Thunder's birth had created a bridge between us now over that cold, rushing river, but who would it cross it, and how?

On a heavy sigh, Grace buried her face in my chest. "I love you."

I kissed the top of her head, my hand sliding down to her ass. "Love you too, baby."

"Daddy, you're touching Mommy's butt again!" Thunder laughed out loud.

"She touched mine first, bud."

Our son burst into giggles, and my heart flew.

"I like Mommy's butt," I said, kneading Grace's ass hard. She squealed and jumped in my hold, and Thunder laughed even harder. "But you know what I like better?"

"Uh oh," said Grace.

Thunder's eyes widened at his mother's ominous tone. "What?"

"*Your* butt!" I chased him, and he hooted as I tackled him, tossed him in the air, and squashed him in my arms.

"Daddy!" He laughed from deep inside his little body. "Daddy!"

"Now Daddy's home, Christmas can begin," Grace said.

Thunder's face beamed. Pure elation.

"We have plenty of wood, so get to fixing the fire, you two," said Grace.

Thunder helped me pile the small and large logs and reset the fire that had petered out.

"Ohhh," Thunder stood before the hearth, his smiling face awash in a blaze of orange-gold as the flames licked at the wood, crackling and popping.

"Pour the wine, baby," I called out to Grace who was busy in the kitchen.

"You sure you don't want a beer?" Grace asked. "After the day you've had?"

"No, sweetheart. Tonight's special, and I want your wine."

She grinned and brought us both beautiful round crystal glasses filled with dark red wine. "There you go."

She'd made me try her favorite Cabernet a year ago—warm, rich, flavorful. I'd liked it. A mellow warmth that pooled in my veins and settled in my chest. Wine's warmth inspired the I-love-you-so-damn-much-my-heart-is-bursting-and-I-need-to-fuck-you-slow-and-sweet-right-now-baby side of my brain. Beer more inspired the I-need-to-pound-you-right-the-fuck-now side of my brain.

We clinked glasses and sipped, our eyes lingering on each other. Her smile grew wider. She liked that we were both drinking out of the fine crystal glasses Tania had gotten her for Christmas last year. This wasn't Grace drinking her wine from her fancy glass and me sucking on my bottle of brew. Nope. We drank together. I liked it. Her tongue swiped at her wet bottom lip.

"That's good, huh?" she murmured, appraising the wine's color.

"Real good."

Just you wait. She'd get her present from me later on tonight, and I couldn't wait to give it to her. I brushed her sweet mouth with mine, and she let loose a small sigh, her lips trembling. I cradled her face. Grace's beautiful hazel eyes were filled with water.

"My kisses still make you emotional, babe?"

"Hmm."

"What is it?"

"It's nothing." She forced her lips to curl up, but I knew my wife.

"Babe."

"I get all sentimental around the holidays."

"I know you do. You got a little quiet there when you and the girls were cleaning up after Thanksgiving dinner at Butler and Tania's."

"You noticed?"

"Of course I did."

"It's just that someone was missing at the cleanup. Someone who always used to organize us in the kitchen. I can still hear her complain that no one knows how to properly load a dishwasher but her." Her smile wobbled.

"It's Ruby's birthday today, I forgot."

She twisted her lips, a tear escaping. "Her having a Christmas birthday made it an even more special holiday. Ruby's birthday would kick off Christmas for us when we were kids—we made it a two day festival of celebrating. When I was on my own, she would come to wherever I lived, and we'd do her birthday and Christmas together. Even after she got married to Alex and had Jake, they would come. We always had this holiday together, even in the shit times." She wiped at her eyes. "And now that you and I have Thunder, she's not here." Her voice ached and my heart hurt. "She should be here. I want her here."

I held my wife tighter. "I know, baby. She should be."

She swallowed. "The smell of candy canes, the ornaments on our tree, that one angel that was her favorite—" she gestured at the beautiful statue of an angel in a purple and gold gown blowing a brass horn sitting on our dining room table on a gold runner. "They're all Ruby to me." Grace blew out a huff of air, her hand curling into my shirt. "And Wreck should be here, too. He'd be the best grandpa ever. It hurts, literally hurts that Thunder is missing out on his aunt and his great uncle."

She was right. It did literally hurt that my big brother wasn't here to see me with my own family, for him to look into Thunder's eyes and see his own. No, they weren't the same color eyes, but Thunder's eyes had a resolve and tenacity that was all Wreck. I wanted him to hear his nephew's hearty laugh, to see him running through the house that was once his. The house he'd brought me to long, long ago.

"And for the first time ever," Grace continued, "I couldn't get to the cemetery with all the snow, I was afraid I'd get stuck there. I always go on her birthday and leave holly branches for her and mom, and one for Dig, and for Wreck."

"I know, babe. We'll go once the roads clear up, first thing." I rubbed a hand down her back. "You miss Jake, too."

"It's our first Christmas without him and Alex, but I'm happy that Alex finally has a serious girlfriend, and this is their first vacation with Jake and her daughter—Christmas in Miami."

After Ruby had passed away, it had taken Alex a while to date again, let alone enter a relationship. I was so happy that he was finally letting himself have a second chance. My second chance had certainly been worth the risk. It was everything.

"I'm glad my Dad's going to spend the weekend with them to see Jake. And I talked to Jake this morning. He said palm trees lit up with Christmas lights are the coolest thing ever."

"That's just too weird," I said. "I wouldn't trade being snowed in here with you and our son for anything in the world."

"Me either." She grinned through the tears sliding down her face. I wiped them away.

"Where is our boy? Things got real quiet all of a sudden."

"Probably in his room, he's been huddling in his teepee all afternoon. He told me he was busy organizing."

"Organizing? Thunder?"

"I thought he'd be more stir crazy waiting for you to get home, but he's been keeping himself busy most of the day."

My gaze darted down the hall which led to our bedrooms. All clear. "Get over here." I pulled my old lady down to the floor and brought her into my lap. Cradling her face, I nipped at her lips, my tongue invading her mouth, our wine blooming. "Fuck, you taste good."

"Shh," she said, pressing against me, her fingers brushing my face. I devoured the smile from her lips and made it mine.

"So when will Santa bring the presents?" came Thunder's booming voice.

I lost my wife's lips as she pulled away.

"Actually honey, come here. Sit down with us." Grace slid back from me, and we settled Thunder in between us. "With all this snow, I'm not sure if Santa's going to make it."

"But everyone knows that Santa rides a sleigh, and sleighs are for snow. And he's got all the reindeer and Rudolph too."

"Right, Rudolph," I murmured, brushing a hand through my hair.

"I know, baby," said Grace. "But Mrs. Claus just sent out a text to all the mommies and daddies here in South Dakota telling us that since the snow is so bad, especially here in Meager, Santa's going to do his best to come, but he might not be able to get through tonight. He has a big responsibility to all the other children around the world, so he's going to go visit them first since they don't have all the snow we do. And after he's done all the way around the world, if the storm's cleared up by then, he'll come to South Dakota."

"Oh."

"Yeah." Grace shot me her daddy-backup-needed-now look.

"South Dakota has the most intense snow, bud. You know that," I said.

Thunder nodded his head.

"Honey, it doesn't mean he's not coming, he's just coming a little later than usual," I said.

""kay." He chewed on his lip.

"When he does come—and we don't know when—it's going to be an amazing surprise, right?" said Grace. "That's exciting, isn't it?"

My girl was good. Always putting a positive spin on shit.

Thunder twisted his little mouth, his head slanting.

"And you love surprises, don't you?" I said.

"Yeah."

"And you know, Santa. He's going to make it up to you in a big way," said Grace. "I'm sure his sack will be stuffed with extra treats for all the good boys and girls who are waiting so patiently here in Meager."

"Hmm," was Thunder's only reply.

"Time for food. Are you hungry, Thunder? Because I have a mean collection of steak, and quesadillas, and piggies in blankets, and cheesy potatoes. All our favorites."

"Piggies!" whooped Thunder.

"I say we eat in here in front of the fire, picnic style, what do you think?" I said.

"I thought picnics were for summer?" asked Thunder.

"We can do whatever we want," I said.

"Christmas picnic! Yay!"

Grace brought out the first platters of food to the living room where Thunder was attempting to set a tablecloth on our cocktail table, but the fabric kept sliding left and right and he let out a huge huff. I helped him get the tablecloth on right, and I put Christmas carols on the stereo. Grace brought out the rest of the food as I placed our big square pillows on the floor around the table for us to sit on.

We settled in, I poured more wine. Grace and I clinked glasses. "Merry Christmas, sweetheart."

Thunder raised his fork in the air. "Merry Christmas!"

2

MILLER

WE'D EATEN. We'd pigged out. All three of us were stretched on the floor.

"I can't believe I ate the whole thing," I said on a groan.

"Do you remember that commercial?" Grace said. "That was a good commercial. A classic from the seventies."

"For an antacid, right? It was Wreck's favorite. He'd rub his stomach and say, "I can't believe I ate the whoooooole thing." I laughed, my brother's voice imitating the ad filling my head.

"Daddy, look at my hat," Thunder sported a red baseball cap with a white mustang patch sewn onto it.

"Where did you get this?" I took my high school cap off his head.

"I found it," he said.

"Found it? Where? I haven't seen this since I don't know when."

The sudden seriousness of my tone had my son straightening his back as he pointed toward the hallway that led to the mudroom/laundry room. "In the box."

"The box?"

"Oh," said Grace, sitting up. "He means that old trunk you

found in the attic last weekend that we haven't had a chance to go through yet. I'd covered that up in the mudroom. Thunder, you found it?"

Thunder's face flushed red.

"You opened that big black trunk all by yourself?" I asked him.

Our son only nodded.

Resourceful, determined. Burning with curiosity. My boy.

I pulled in a breath. That trunk was an oldie of Wreck's. I didn't know how I'd missed it all these years, but it was stashed in a far corner of the attic under a couple of tarps, behind an old ping-pong table. A pile that I'd kept meaning to get to all these years, but hadn't.

My son stood stock-still waiting for me to pass judgment on another of his hasty actions. I lifted my chin. "Well, you going to show us what you found inside?"

"Oh, hang on." Grace popped a red Santa cap on his head, pulling the tail up. "You're Santa's helper tonight. Bring it on. Surprise us."

A huge grin split his face as he charged down the hallway, his sock-covered feet stamping furiously on the wood. He quickly returned holding a pile of magazines and wearing a huge athletic jacket with white sleeves and a big red M patch on the front.

"Holy crap, that's my varsity letter jacket from high school," I said, fingering a cracked leather sleeve.

"Lookin' good, LeBeau," said Grace, her fingers brushing the patch with the red mustang on it, my number patched on the other side. "I remember Daddy wearing this in high school. Red looked good on him, too. He was a really good football player."

Thunder beamed, stood up straighter, but the jacket was heavy, and his shoulders slumped. Grace adjusted the jacket on him.

"What else you got there, bud? Comic books?" I asked, and Thunder handed me the comics he held.

"Any Archie? Betty and Veronica?" laughed Grace.

"No, babe. Sorry. Batman, X-men, Silver Surfer. Dang, I thought these had gotten thrown away." I shuffled through the colorful vintage comics. "Once in a while Wreck would take me to Rapid on a Saturday morning to check out this shop a friend of his had with old comics and collectibles. It was the best." My hand pressed over the wrinkled ends of a Batman comic as Thunder ran back to his room.

He brought me a couple of black pencils, a stained box of charcoals, another one of pastels. "Jeez, my first art supplies," I murmured.

"I found something else too," said Thunder. The kid looked like he would burst any second.

"Let's see," I said.

Thunder skirted the sofa, charging back down the hallway and returned clutching a small brown stuffed animal. "Look! Look! It's a fuffalo!"

"Fuffa-what?" I asked. His face flushed, he held up a small, furry, brown stuffed animal for my inspection.

"A little buffalo." I stroked the thick brown fur of the toy. The furry creature's small tail was coming apart from his body. I tugged on it gently, and a prickle swept over my skin.

"He's so cute," said Grace.

"I like my fuffalo," said Thunder.

I fingered the toy's little horns, his shaggy mane and let out a breath.

"He looks like those classic souvenirs they sell," said Grace. "I remember seeing those little buffaloes at Wall Drug when I was a kid, but all my parents got us were wooden Buffalo nickels and stamped pennies."

I blinked, my mouth dried. Something, something from far away tugged at my insides as I took in the buffalo's velvety face, his black hooves, those curved horns. Something I couldn't place with logic and sense, but my heart knew. I knew. "This was my buffalo when I was a kid, Thunder."

"Really?" asked Grace. "You had it when you came to Meager? But you were a teenager then."

"No, I think I was much younger when I had it. I don't know."

Thunder carefully brushed the buffalo's tail with a fingertip. "His tail's coming off. Can you fix it, Daddy?"

"Yeah, I can fix it. I think I'm the one who ripped it."

"You did?" my son said.

"I remember holding him by the tail and spinning him around..." my thoughts trailed off. That buffalo clutched in my son's hands now hurtled me back to a time when my heart had been wrenched, changing it forever. My mother's glaring sunlight gone, replaced by my grandmother's silent warmth.

"Now that's a real man toy," said Grace, and Thunder's eyes lit up. "You missed it, Miller—the other day when Jill brought Becca and Nicky over to play, Becca put her Barbie in Thunder's train."

"Oh no," I said.

"And then she put makeup on her Barbie," said Grace. "That's when the pooper hit the fan."

"Oh boy."

"Pooper!" Thunder broke out into laughter.

"Pooper dooper," said Grace, planting a kiss on Thunder's cheek. "Why don't you take the jacket off now, Thunder, and I'll clean it up for you this week, okay?" She slid my old jacket off Thunder's little body and laid it on the side of the couch. "Babe? You okay?"

"Yeah. Just wondering why Wreck had this. I think I remember the toy, but as one of those flash memories from when I was really young."

"How young?"

"Like with my mother young."

"Oh, three, four years old?"

"Like me?" asked Thunder.

I was three when my mother gave me up. That day the earth dried, the sun changed color, and flavors altered—flavors I came to love, because they were me, my blood, my fabric. But at three, I only knew my mother was no more. She'd quit. I would never hear her voice again, feel her arms holding me. Thank God my son would never know such upheaval.

"I don't remember having it at the res though, with my dad and my grandma. I'm not sure now," I said.

Thunder plucked the toy from me. "Now it's my fuffalo, Daddy."

"That's right." I tousled my son's long dark hair as he hugged my lost buffalo. "He's yours now. Uncle Wreck kept him safe for you all these years."

"I love him," said Thunder planting a kiss on the buffalo, squeezing him.

"Ah, you see, Thunder?" said Grace. "Santa may not make it tonight to our house, but, boy, Uncle Wreck was watching out for you, right? I told you, surprises where you least expect them."

I caught my wife's bright gaze and held it. God, I loved this woman.

"I think now's the perfect time to read "T'was the Night Before Christmas" together. I'll go get it." Grace went to Thunder's room to get the book.

Thunder propped his little buffalo on the table and made roaring sounds. "Remember the fuffaloes we saw in the snow last week, Daddy? That was so cool."

Last week on the way to Rapid we'd seen a herd tromping through the perfect white drifts, and Thunder had gotten so excited. Rugged, huge animals, their heavy fur covered in frost and icy drips of snow, seemingly unbothered by the harsh elements. No, they were in their element. They belonged here.

Like us.

Thunder said, "Now I have my own fuffalo."

3

GRACE

WE'D PILED the dishes in the dishwasher, left the pans to soak in the sink, abandoned our wine glasses on the counter. And of course, chocolate milk and gingerbread cookies which Tania's mom, Rae had given us, were in a bright red dish waiting for Santa to bite into should he happen to make it to our house this evening.

Miller brought Thunder to his bed, and the moment my husband entered our bedroom and laid eyes on me sitting in the leather arm chair in a snow white Lenore's Lace corset style nightie he clicked the door closed behind him and remained glued to the spot.

I spread my legs. "Get over here."

His gruff grunt reached me in the dark like a heat seeking laser and my clit throbbed, my pulse kicking up even more speed than when I'd flung myself in the chair waiting for him to walk inside. Miller stalked over and got down on his knees before me, warm hands slowly sliding up my bare thighs, taking my breath away. *This man.*

"Fuck me," he muttered, his thumbs brushing over the delicate fabric between my legs.

"Merry Merry, baby," I breathed.

He snapped at the thin strap which lay over a nipple, and I gasped at the sting. "Is this some kind of modern Victorian bondage extravaganza?"

"Lenore's Lace style."

"I never get tired of these creations of hers."

"Neither do I."

He snapped the taut strap which lay over my other nipple, and the prick of the sting lit another match in my veins. Miller bent his head, and his warm wet tongue swirled over the hardened nub, his teeth brushing over the delicate flesh as he sucked roughly.

"Oh, yes."

"I'm going to give you your present now." His hand cupped a breast roughly, and I gasped. "It's a two parter."

"A two parter?" I said.

He got up and opened the leather pouch he'd taken with him on his trip and fished out a small gift box. "For my lady," he handed it to me, getting back on his knees in front of me.

Jewelry. I loved jewelry, a certain type of jewelry, and he loved gifting it to me. His eyes gleamed, his anticipation making my pulse throb faster.

"Open it, baby." His fingers slid down my middle to between my legs, cupping me, his heat blazing over my skin, his low voice whispering in my ear, "Then I'll unwrap you." He snapped open the tiny snaps between my legs.

I let out a ragged breath and tore off the ribbon and opened the small suede box. "Oh, Miller." I stared at the piece. He took the eternity band out of the box and slid it over my other stacked rings on my finger from our engagement and wedding, planting a kiss on the rings.

"It's all of our birthstones with diamonds. All together on one ring." He'd already given me a ring of only amethysts—our son's birthstone—after Thunder was born, but now a ring for me with all of us on it.

"It's perfect." I kissed him. "I love it."

He took a breast in his mouth and sucked and nipped at my flesh as he stroked up and down my wet core. A groan escaped him as two of his fingers slid inside me, curling against my wall, thrusting, his thumb stroking my clit. My hips rocked to his rhythm as he greedily kneaded a breast.

"Oh, oh, Miller—"

He released me. "You know what I want, baby."

He liked to watch me.

My one foot planted itself on his chest and pushed. A heated grin tugged at his mouth as his hand slid up around my raised thigh. I stroked between my legs, his fingers burning a trail on my inner thigh as I brought myself closer and closer to the edge under his searing dark gaze. My head fell back, my body arched with the building pleasure and suddenly, he kissed my bare foot and stood up.

My pulse careened as he ripped off his henley, loosened his sweats, tugged them down and kicked them off along with his socks. Naked before me, he pulled on his erect shaft, rubbing himself up and down as he watched me, his breathing ragged, heavy, matching my own.

Something glinted in the dim light of the room, and I blinked.

"Is that a—you got a—No."

He chuckled darkly as he pulled on his gorgeous cock, making the silver ring at the base of his shaft visible. "For you. This one's sized perfectly." He pulled hard on his stiff length.

"Baby!"

"It's feels real different from the rubber one you'd gotten us to play with."

"But I thought you didn't like it. You said it felt weird, uncomfortable. I thought—"

"But *you* liked it." He stroked his hard, hard cock, and I blinked, my heart squeezed. He was killing me, and I burned this image of him in my brain. My man staring at me with wild lust roaring in his full dark eyes along with the pleasure he felt at surprising me, giving me what I wanted. I had no words. His hand curled tighter, moved faster over his dick in preparation to take me, conquer me, make my wishes come true. "Didn't you like it, baby?"

My heart banged in my chest at his gruff, harsh tone. "I liked it. A lot."

He smiled. A smile that was full of planned surprises and devilish satisfaction. "I asked Ronny about them because he does piercings at his shop, so I figured—"

Ronny was the best tattoo artist in the Black Hills, and Miller and all the Jacks only got their tattoos from him. And now that Ronny was in a serious relationship with Alicia, she'd convinced him to open a shop here in Meager.

Miller said, "He showed me which were the best and sized it to perfection."

I licked my lips. "Sized it?"

"So I feel good about it being on me. And you know what? I like the feel of it." He pumped at himself faster. "All tight right where it counts. Tight and hard for you."

"You're killing me."

"That's the idea."

"Miller—"

"I got a vibrating attachment we can try too."

"Holy shit."

"Another layer of crazy for my woman."

"Miller."

"The rubber felt weird on me, but I did like the pressure, and coming did feel stronger."

I swallowed hard remembering the crazy sensations of that sex session. "Hmm." I sat up straighter on the chair, licking my lips like some desperate, hungry young vampire watching her prey cavort before her, beckon her.

"You make me horny as fuck all hours of the day and night," he said on a groan.

My insides throbbed. "Me too, baby," I breathed.

"I want a thicker, fuller, and longer lasting hard-on for you, Grace, because I want to make my woman's fantasies come true."

I'm done.

I slid my hands up his legs at those words, at that dark tone shading his deep voice, and I pulled him close, sucked on his balls. He let out a low grunt, digging a hand in my hair as my tongue flirted with the ring, lavishing it with long and short licks.

Suddenly I was being lifted and jammed against the wall. I gasped, my legs curling instinctively around his solid hips, clawing at his rock hard body as his cock slid up and down my wetness, the cool hard texture of the ring grazing me mercilessly.

"You feel that?"

"What the hell is that?" I groaned.

"Ridges and bumps on the ring."

"Holy crap."

"Custom made for my sweet, hot pussy," he murmured thickly on a deep thrust.

Oh.

My.

Fuck.

"Miller!"

My fingernails dug into his neck, and a large, warm hand gripped my ass, keeping me close, keeping me pinned to the wall as he pulled out and thrust deeper, faster. He circled, I cried out.

So full, so full.

Our damp skin sliding, our groans urged each other on. His warm scent, our sweat and musk filled my senses. The hard wall at my back and his steely grip kept me focused and bound to his demanding need. I met his pounding with poundings of my own.

"Come get me. Come get me, baby," he pleaded, he urged through gritted teeth.

I was bound, I was free. I gave, I took. Our bodies shuddered together. A hand suddenly dug into my hair, yanking hard, his hips meeting mine, our mouths devouring each other as our hearts stopped.

And started once more.

Miller carried me to our bed, our slick, spent bodies tangled in one another. "Love you, Grace," he whispered hoarsely against my throat.

Wiping his long hair back, I brushed his sweaty forehead with a kiss. "Can we make that a new holiday tradition?"

His fingers slid between my ass cheeks. "What's that? A new toy every Christmas Eve for Mommy and Daddy?"

My legs squeezed around one of his rock hard thighs, a hand going to his man jewelry, sliding it off. "Yes, please. The possibilities are endless."

4

MILLER

I COULDN'T SLEEP.

I went to check on Thunder, but he wasn't in his bed. He was all curled up in his blanket with the buffalo inside his teepee. Lowering myself to the floor next to him, I rubbed my son's back, his little breaths hitching, releasing. Doing this always reminded me of when he was a newborn and I'd stroke his back as he'd slept in his crib to feel his lungs working, his heart beating, the rhythms electrifying. A miracle.

My gaze went to the mural on his walls that I'd painted for him when he was born. A soaring eagle, a charging hawk. A herd of wild mustangs thundering across the prairie grasses, and a herd of buffaloes lumbering across a hill on another wall. Tall, green gold grasses, a white goat perched on a granite mountain by a waterfall, a great blue sky heavy with puffs of clouds.

In another lifetime, Thunder's room had been my bedroom.

When Wreck had first brought me to Meager from the reservation and shown me this room, the bedroom that was meant for me, I'd seen a simmer of anxiety and anticipation on his face that had made me swallow hard as I stood in the doorway. Those dark-blue eyes of his trained on me, waiting for my reaction, bracing for the worst. Dig and Boner stood behind us in the hallway shifting their weight, their boots scraping on the wood floor as I took in the room.

Oh, I'd inhaled every detail before me. I closed my eyes, seeing every detail again.

Freshly painted white walls. A big double bed with lots of plump pillows and a thick dark blue comforter with tan stripes, and curtains that freaking matched. An old wood desk with a metal lamp on it and a couple of pencils in a container ready to be used. A small television on top of a pine dresser. My insides vibrated. It was Wreck trying his best. It was Wreck giving a shit and showing me he cared. He'd made a decision, he'd come and got me and was all in.

A tidal wave of warmth surged in my chest threatening to drown me, and it was then that I knew. I was sure that the dull hell of the last few years was finally over. That my grandmother had been right all the times she'd told me there were always second chances to be had, and I needed to believe and be ready to embrace them when they happened, that's what made them real. But then she'd died, and I was sure any hope of those second chances for me was done.

Hoping was a fanciful fairy. Reality, though, that brittle, bleak bitch I'd stared in the eyes was a sure thing.

My gaze shot to the doorway of Thunder's room where another lifetime ago Wreck and I and Dig and Boner had once stood. Me on the edge of a new world. This bedroom was a palace of second chances to me, an oasis of hope. A new territory unlike any other I'd ever known.

Then came those three words in his deep voice suddenly gentle, quiet, almost uncertain.

"You like it?" Wreck said.

My mind blanked, my vision blurred. My lips parted to answer, but my throat burned, my lungs tightened, and no words came out. What words would have been right? Only that ring of heat in my heart that was my grandmother squeezed hard.

Too much, too colorful, too big. Somewhere between painful and oh so beautiful.

I buried my face in my brother's chest, my hands gripping his back. He grunted, wrapping his arms around me, holding me fast against his body, a hand in my hair as one sob after the next hiccuped out of me. He held me and didn't let go.

"You're home now, bud. You got that? You're home."

Home.

Now I'd made this home my family's home. He'd given me that.

I'd managed to bring two things from my grandmother's house in Pine Ridge before we went flying out of there—my favorite photo of her as a young woman, her hair long, a feather in it, beads around her neck as she danced at a tribal festival, her fierce eyes caught by the camera as she pivoted. That was now framed in silver and on the mantle of the fireplace. And the beaded dream-catcher she'd given me now hung over Thunder's bed.

A warmth bubbled through my veins, a smile tugged on my lips. I scooped up Thunder all wrapped up in his blanket. Something small flopped to the floor. The buffalo. I leaned down and nabbed it, and brought my son to the living room, settling him into the corner of our big sectional sofa. I tucked the buffalo back into his arms, and he let out a deep sigh.

The embers still glowed red gold, the ash simmered white, and I added more small logs and one big one to get it going again. I turned on the Christmas tree lights, and the two ceramic Christmas village houses Grace had set up on a small table to which Thunder had added three of his toy motorcycles. Sitting on the floor, my back leaning against the sofa, I stroked my son's head, my fingers finding the buffalo's soft fur.

That buffalo.

I did remember it right along with my mother's face, for some reason. Her forced smiles that convinced us all everything would be fine. She had a plan. And I remembered my dad's unsmiling face from back then, his stern features. Muscular long legs in snug jeans, and those boots. A dark brown pair of Tony Lama's, as brown as at the buffalo's fur. He kept them clean and shiny, and they always looked brand new. His steps were heavy and distinct in those boots, I remember the sound on my Grandmother's peeling linoleum floor in that tiny kitchen of hers. I'd wanted to grow up and wear jeans and Tony Lamas too.

The flames crackled sharply licking the top of the hearth in a frenzied dance.

No, this buffalo never made it to Grandma Kim's at Pine Ridge. There'd been other toys there. A few good ones. Some handmade, others clunky metal trucks and plastic guns. Small rubbery farm animals and plastic soldiers. I remembered one stuffed animal that had kept me company in my narrow thin bed, a Snoopy whose white fur had gone grey and his ears had frayed. But no, not this buffalo.

Thunder rolled over and stretched out, curling his little body again into the corner of the sofa.

I grinned. How many times had Wreck and I sat on this sofa and watched a movie or a ball game devouring impossibly huge sandwiches or giant pizzas loaded with everything? Too many to count.

I went to our bedroom. "Grace? Baby, wake up."

"What is it? Is Thunder okay?"

"He's fine." I swept her hair from her face. "Come with me."

"Did Santa make it?"

I let out a laugh. "Come on."

Her hair tousled, wearing my thick fleece black bathrobe over the flannel pj's she'd changed into before falling asleep, Grace shuffled into the living room, her face lighting up at the sight of the fire. "Perfect." She settled onto the floor next to me, adjusting the blanket over Thunder.

"This is the place to be on Christmas Eve," she said.

"It is perfect."

"The tree is exceptional this year, sweetheart," she said, eyeing the huge fir in the corner of the great room, a glowing concoction of twinkling red lights and a rich cascade of ornaments.

"Mine and Wreck's Christmas trees were usually ridiculously tall, usually uneven, and scraped the ceiling. We'd get all enthusiastic about finding a great tree, but we'd forget about measuring it so that it would fit into the house, through the door, not to mention the room. Most times, they wouldn't fit, but we didn't care. We'd chopped it and lugged it home ourselves. That made it special. So there we'd be sawing the poor thing here and a little bit there, leaving it uneven. Oh man. We never had enough ornaments, just whatever colored glass balls we could get at a convenience store. We always meant to get more "next year," but we'd never get around to it. A ton of lights and tinsel dripping off the branches did the trick for us just fine."

Our tree had ornaments that Grace's grandparents and parents had passed on to her, along with ones we'd bought on our first Christmas together. Then there was the small frame decorated with holly berry trim in which I'd tucked a photo of baby Thunder with Santa his first year.

"That first Christmas I was here," I said. "Wreck got me that fancy set of German sketching pencils, charcoals, and pastels Thunder found today. From a real art store in Denver."

"He did?"

"Yeah. He signed me up for a serious art class in Rapid after that. It was pretty great, I learned all the right basics. But then football took over."

"A man of so many talents." She leaned her head against my arm.

I was real glad Grace and I stayed on here in Wreck's house.

That the renovation I'd begun alone we'd seen through together, building a small addition to add the man cave and extra room for family or friends to spend the night, the porch Grace had wanted, rebuilding the garage. And over the past several years, Grace had added her touches, her mark for our family. Her love, her personality, her joy. She'd made this house hum in a way it never had before, the way a house should.

I would have liked to have seen Wreck here with his own family—old lady, kids. He'd put energy into saving details of our existence and those of others, of "the quiet, unsung treasures," as he'd call them. If he and his one love, Isi had had a chance, how different would this house have been?

Isi had gotten killed just before he'd brought me to Meager. I'd heard things around the clubhouse, I'd seen the lipstick knife of hers he'd saved and kept in his dresser drawer. I'd asked questions, but his answers had been brusque, evasive. One day at the shop, Dig had shaken his head at me and said, "He doesn't talk about it, Mill. Not ever, he can't. The hurt's too deep. You need to leave it."

And so I left it.

Grace brushed a hand through my hair bringing me back to the here and now of our Christmas Eve. She gave me that soft smile that was just for me.

I slid my forehead against hers. "Missed you when I was away."

"Me too," she whispered. "I don't like being apart. Not even for an overnight business trip. Silly, I know, but—"

"No, it's not. I feel the same."

She melted against me, and I pulled my wife into my lap, my lips nuzzling her neck. Without Wreck, there would have been no Grace. No Thunder.

I took in a breath, my eyelids jamming shut. *Because without Wreck there'd be no me.*

Wreck and I never discussed it, I never discussed it with

anyone. It cut deep and was over, done with, the past. Just like whatever he'd gone through with his lover. We both marched forward, side by side.

Grace and I held each other and watched the fire, the sound of our son's even breathing wrapping around us like a blanket. "I always loved Christmas," said Grace. "The caroling, going to the tree lighting in Rapid, baking all sorts of goodies and gifting them to our teachers, our neighbors, family. Finding just the right gift for everyone on your list, wrapping them up special, hiding them until the right moment. Charlie Brown, the Grinch, and the Little Drummer Boy on TV. But then suddenly, Christmas Day would arrive, Ruby and I would open our presents, we'd eat, and then that was it, it was all downhill from there."

"Downhill?" I laughed.

"I don't mean the presents. I mean the feeling, the spirit of the holiday. You don't realize it because it happens so quickly. There at Christmas dinner, the holiday has already deflated by then. *Phht*, that's it. Everything suddenly loses its sparkle and becomes ordinary again."

"Ordinary," I repeated.

Grace wrapped an arm around my shoulders. "The older I get, the more sentimental I'm becoming. Time passing is more real to me now that it ever has been before. But with Thunder, we get to make his Christmas experience sparkle. Make new memories for us, for him."

I let out a chuckle. "Then he'll feel sentimental about it all one day."

"That's right," Grace whispered, emotion coloring her voice as she slid a warm hand in mine. "And he has different things to enjoy than we did. The club toy drive for the hospital, Meager's first Christmas bazaar this year, those beautiful big Santa cookies Erica bakes at the Meager Grand along with the candy cane hot chocolate. Our Jacks family. Tighter than ever."

"The gift grab-bag with the kids at the club was insane this year."

"Oh Lord." Grace laughed. "I remember everyone used to make Jump dress up as Santa because he always had the biggest belly. He hated it, and every year would refuse to do it, but in the end, he'd always give in and end up enjoying it."

"Yeah, with a fifth of vodka under his belt."

"Bear is into it without the booze. He's a good Santa."

"Santa? Did Santa come?" rose Thunder's voice from behind us.

"Not yet, honey."

"Oh." He plopped back onto the cushion. "Are we all sleeping here tonight?"

"Yes, baby, we're waiting for him together," said Grace. "I'm going to get the big down comforter and our pillows. Christmas Eve slumber party. A new tradition."

"Mommy, make us a tent."

The three of us slept in the living room before the fire, cuddled up with each other, waiting for Santa, and making a sparkling memory.

5

MILLER

A LOUD NOISE had me flinching under the sweet warmth of the comforter. Was someone banging on the door?

The front bell dinged.

"Santa! Santa's here!" Thunder scrambled to his feet and clambered over us, a bullet. He hopped at the front door. "Come on, Daddy. Open the door!"

"Hold on, bud." I lifted up from the pile of the thick comforter and made my way to the door, rubbing at my eyes at the morning sunlight filling the house. I peered through the glass window at the top of the door, and my pulse shot up. "Holy crap."

"Who is it?" Grace asked.

Quickly unlocking the door, I swung it open. "Dad."

There at the foot of my front steps holding a small shopping bag in the blinding glare of the sun on the white, white snow stood Jason LeBeau, his pickup truck up on a bank of snow. "Hey there," he said, releasing a deep breath, his dark eyes squinting, holding mine. "Merry Christmas."

"Dad."

Another gray haired man appeared on my walkway. Ray, Grace's dad. "Merry Christmas, son."

"Grandpa! Grandpa!" shouted Thunder from behind my legs. "It's Grandpa and Grandpa!" Thunder hopped up and down.

"Merry Christmas." I swung the front door open wide. "Come on in."

Holding onto the railing, Jason limped up the stone steps. His fall from a horse from a few years back had left its mark on him. Ray followed him into the house.

"Jason? So glad you came," Grace said, giving my father a hug. "Dad!" She hugged her father. "What are you doing here? I thought you were going to Miami."

Ray Hastings kept an arm around his daughter. "I couldn't leave, Gracie. I heard that tremor in your voice when I called you the day before and we talked about your sister's birthday."

"You didn't have to—"

"Yes, baby girl, I did," Ray said.

She hugged her father again.

"I decided to surprise you," Ray said. "And when you told me how you didn't get a chance to....you know—" his eyes darted down at Thunder "—lock up properly at Eagle Wings. I figured since I have that spare set of keys you all had given me in case of emergencies, I could go over and check myself."

"Right," Grace murmured, her eyes wide.

"This was an emergency, in my book. The snow stopped late last night, so first thing this morning, I managed to follow the plow, got through in my SUV, and went up there and—"

"And?"

"I locked up proper." Ray handed her the keys to his car.

Grace fisted his keys, a huge grin on her face. "Thank you."

"You bet." Ray grinned back.

Thunder crashed into Ray's legs. "Hey, Thunder." Ray crouched down. "Give your Grandpa a hug." Thunder hugged him, and Ray lifted him up, settling him on his waist. "You see how I brought Grandpa Jason with me? Isn't that lucky?"

Thunder only nodded, staring at Jason. He'd only seen him a

couple of times before. Jason was quiet, spoke little, and had stern lines etched in his tan, weathered face. He fascinated Thunder.

"I'm going to get dressed," said Grace, plucking the pillows and the comforter from the living room floor. "I'll be right back to make us coffee." She darted down the hall to our bedroom.

"Dad," I said. "I thought you didn't want to travel with the storm coming on."

"Changed my mind and didn't give up. Being stubborn as well as impulsive got me up to Dead Ringers yesterday afternoon before things got real bad, and I stayed at the motel across the way. By morning they'd cleared a section of the highway there, and I managed to get into Meager. It was slow going, but I ended up following a plow once I got into town, and there was Ray in front of me."

Ray took Thunder into the living room, and Jason's heavy gaze met mine. "I was wrong to say no to your invitation, Miller. I used the storm as an excuse. It's Christmas, and to be here with you and Grace and the little one is mighty special. I had to come." His eyes tensed for a moment. This was hard for him.

"Come on in," I said. "Have a seat."

"We had a slumber party last night. Right here," said Thunder pointing to the living room floor.

"You did?" said Ray, settling Thunder on the sofa next to him. Jason sat on his grandson's other side.

"We were waiting for Santa," said Thunder.

"Did you see him?" asked Jason.

Thunder shook his head.

"Oh, that's too bad. Well, I got something for you." Jason lifted the paper shopping bag he'd brought in with him. He took out a wrapped gift and gave it to Thunder. "Merry Christmas, Thunder."

Thunder's face brightened and he ripped at the paper, revealing a long wood box with an engraving of the Lakota star on it. "Careful, son. Let me open it for you." Jason flipped up the small brass latch on the polished box, opening the cover. A long feather lay inside. "It's a feather from the great golden eagle," Jason said.

My insides tightened. Thunder stilled, both of us staring at the feather.

"My daddy gave it to me," said my father. "It was from his pa, and his pa before him."

"Grandma had told me about it," I said. "But she didn't know where it was. She used to fret about it. She thought you'd—"

"Oh, I had it safe," he said, a gleam in his eye. "She worried too much." He let out a breath. "I'm sorry that I never got the chance to give it to your daddy like I should have, Thunder. But I'm very glad that I can give it to you now."

Thunder's eyes popped open even wider, and they found mine, asking for approval. I nodded at him, and he smiled softly at me, at his grandfather.

"That is incredible," murmured Ray. "You like it, Thunder?"

"Can I touch it?" he asked.

"Careful now, go on," Jason said. "It's very old, very delicate."

Thunder lightly stroked the spine of the feather, his lips forming an O. "We see eagles in the sky sometimes."

"An eagle is the strongest and bravest of all birds," said my father. "He's considered a holy messenger of the Creator. A feather from the great eagle was an honor earned by warriors who showed bravery, loyalty, and strength in battle. If they collected enough, they'd make headdresses with them that were worn with dignity and pride."

Jason took the feather out of the box and held it over Thunder's head, and my pulse drummed. A good wish passed down from fathers to sons. A blessing. My heart thudded in my chest at the wonder stamped on my son's face as he stared up at the feather. From father to son to father to son. My heart clenched with an impossible emotion.

"I wish you bravery and happiness, Richard Thunder Kichú

Flies as Eagles," said my father, his voice even, strong. "To everyone in this house, peace, prosperity, and happiness." He placed the feather back in the box and closed it, placing it in his grandson's hands. "This is yours now, Thunder."

I cleared my throat, but my voice still came out hoarse. "We should keep that in a special place, Thunder. Right here, on the tall shelf over the fireplace next to Grandma Kim's picture. When you want to look at it, we'll do it together, okay?"

"Okay, Daddy."

My father met my gaze, and I lifted my chin at him.

"What do you say to Grandpa Jason?" Ray leaned into Thunder, taking the box and placing it on the table.

"Thank you, Grandpa Jason." Thunder hurled himself at my dad, his little arms extended in a hug.

"Oh, you're welcome, son." Jason wrapped his arms around Thunder, his eyes closing, soaking in the moment. "You're very welcome."

"Thunder! Thunder!" Grace yelled from the front yard. "Honey, come see!"

Thunder scrambled off the sofa and ran to the door, and I opened it. Grace stood all bundled up in my winter jacket, a Santa hat, and her winter boots amidst wrapped packages dotting the white blanket of snow.

"Mommy?"

"Honey, Santa came!"Grace jumped up and down in the snow. "He must have been in a big rush to deliver all the presents before everyone woke up, and he missed our chimney, and everything landed in the yard. Come see! Come get your goodies!"

Ray grinned, grabbing Thunder's little snow jacket from the coat rack hooks along the wall and got him into it. "Wait, wait, and your boots—" My son drove his feet into his little rubber boots and charged out the door.

Grace tromped all over the snow, arms waving, pointing. "Over here! And here! Quick, Thunder!"

Thunder squealed and laughed, picking up the boxes and bags gleaming in the morning light, stuck in the snow like red and green candies in a field of sugar.

"You found it?" came my dad's suddenly thin voice behind me. "So long ago."

I turned around. He held the buffalo. "What are you talking about?" I asked.

"This is the buffalo I'd gotten you when you were a baby."

My heart drummed in my chest. "You gave it to me?"

"Yes. You loved it. Always had him with you. You would spin him around by his tail, and it had ripped a little. See?" He fingered the torn edge of the tail. "You always had it with you, every time I came to see you. And then that day when your mother...when I took you home with me, somewhere, somehow you'd lost it. I looked everywhere—in the truck, I'd driven back to the restaurant we'd stopped at, the gas station, but I couldn't find it. You cried and cried. It was terrible. I didn't know what to do. I was upset myself. And so angry. Everything was wrong that day. Everything. But the one right thing was that you were home with me and your grandmother where you belonged." His long fingers stroked the buffalo's head.

My father had given me that toy? My father had been upset over the loss of it on the very day my mother had dumped me on him?

"Where did you find it?" he asked, his voice rough. "You've kept it all this time?" A smile flickered over his face.

"Wreck had it," I said. "Thunder just found it in a trunk Wreck had packed with my stuff from when I was a kid."

"Really? Well. He was there that day."

"He was?"

"Yes." My father let out a heavy breath, his gaze darting around the house. "That's nice that he saved it for you. Very thoughtful."

Thunder and Grace rushed into the house, their arms full of

presents, their faces flushed, the fresh cold air zinging in with them. Ray shut the door, preserving the warmth of our house. Thunder planted himself on the floor surrounded by his presents, and ripped at the paper, flinging ribbons. He did a double take at Jason who still held the buffalo.

"Do you like my fuffalo, Grandpa?"

"I do, Thunder. He's a very fine fuffalo." Jason handed him the toy.

"I think he needs a ribbon too, he didn't get to be wrapped up." Thunder tied a bright red ribbon around the buffalo's head. "That's better. Merry Christmas, fuffalo."

My father's hand gripped the arm of the sofa, his knuckles white. An expression crossed his face that I couldn't define, but pierced at my insides. Jaw clenched, eyes glimmering, the lines of his face deepening. Emotion churned through him and he struggled to reign it in.

Grace slid her arms around my waist. "You good?" she whispered.

I kissed her cold cheek, tightening my arm around her shoulders. "More than good, and very merry."

My gaze shot up to the framed photo on the far wall of the big, tall white guy who'd shown up on the reservation like a mirage in the harsh sunlight. In the photo he wore an old T with the sleeves cut off showing his tattooed covered arms, along with leathers, and forbidding black boots. He stood in a grassy yard amongst motorcycles of all kinds, some in pieces, some whole.

That big man of few words carried an air of sadness with him like the scent of metal, motor oil, and Dial soap that I'd later come to know as uniquely him. But in only this photo, of all the ones I had of him, did he wear a hint of a smile that the photographer had managed to capture.

I smiled back.

THE END

BOOKS BY CAT PORTER

LOCK & KEY

RANDOM & RARE

IRON & BONE

BLOOD & RUST

LOCK & KEY CHRISTMAS

THE DUST AND THE ROAR

FURY

DAGGER IN THE SEA

WOLFSGATE

ABOUT THE AUTHOR

CAT PORTER was born and raised in New York City, but also spent a few years in Texas and Europe along the way, which made her as wanderlusty as her parents. As an introverted, only child, she had very big, but very secret dreams for herself. She graduated from Vassar College, was a struggling actress, an art gallery girl, special events planner, freelance writer, restaurant hostess, and had all sorts of other crazy jobs all hours of the day and night to help make those dreams come true. She has two children's books traditionally published under her maiden name.

She now lives on a beach outside of Athens, Greece with her husband, three children, and a huge Cane Corso, freaks out regularly, still daydreams way too much, and now truly doesn't give AF. She is addicted to reading, classic films, cafés on the beach, the Greek islands, Instagram, Pearl Jam and U2, the whiskey she brought home from Ireland and the bourbon she brought home from Nashville, and realllllly good coffee. Writing has always kept her somewhat sane, extremely happy, and a productive member of society.

for more more more
www.catporter.eu

Sign up for the Cat List
for book news, exclusive content, sales,
special giveaways and offers

Visit Cat's Pinterest boards for the Lock & Key Series and all her books

Join Cat's Facebook group:
Cat Porter's Cat Callers

Email me at catporter103@gmail.com

facebook.com/catporterauthor

twitter.com/catporter103

instagram.com/catporter.writer

amazon.com/author/catporter

bookbub.com/authors/cat-porter

pinterest.com/catporter103

Printed in Great Britain
by Amazon